STRANGE VISIONS

SINKHOLE

STRANGE VISIONS

RONALD B. KLINE JR.

DARBY CREEK
MINNEAPOLIS

A special thank-you to Precious McKenzie for her help in writing this book.

Darby Creek
An imprint of Lerner Publishing Group, Inc.
241 First Avenue North
Minneapolis, MN 55401 USA

For reading levels and more information, look up this title at www.lernerbooks.com.

Cover and interior images: Natsmith1/Shutterstock; Milano M (chapter number background)

Main body text set in Janson Text LT Std.
Typeface provided by Adobe Systems.

Library of Congress Cataloging-in-Publication Data

Names: Kline, Ronald B., Jr., author.
Title: Strange visions / Ronald B. Kline Jr.
Description: Minneapolis : Darby Creek, [2023] | Series: Sinkhole | Audience: Ages 11–18. | Audience: Grades 7–9. | Summary: Seventeen-year-old DJ Porter is worried when the animals and people of her hometown start coming down with a mysterious illness, but the arrival of federal agents and scientists make her wonder if something more is going on in Foggy Creek, Texas.
Identifiers: LCCN 2022025437 (print) | LCCN 2022025438 (ebook) | ISBN 9781728475523 (lib. bdg.) | ISBN 9781728477992 (pbk.) | ISBN 9781728479583 (eb pdf)
Subjects: CYAC: Extraterrestrial beings—Fiction. | Sick—Fiction. | BISAC: YOUNG ADULT FICTION / Paranormal, Occult & Supernatural | YOUNG ADULT FICTION / Animals / Pets | LCGFT: Paranormal fiction. | High interest-low vocabulary books. | Novels.
Classification: LCC PZ7.1.K6535 St 2023 (print) | LCC PZ7.1.K6535 (ebook) | DDC [Fic]—dc23

LC record available at https://lccn.loc.gov/2022025437
LC ebook record available at https://lccn.loc.gov/2022025438

Manufactured in the United States of America
1 – TR – 12/15/22

A faded red pickup truck rolled over Interstate 20. DJ, more properly known as Darlene Jane Porter, was driving. She could hear her father snoring in the passenger's seat. They'd been on the road for days, meeting with ranchers about cattle. He had hoped to expand their herd, but he wanted to get just the right genetics. The best of the best this time, he had told her.

DJ flicked on the windshield wipers. *Ugh*, she thought. Dead lovebugs coated the windshield with slime. The wiper blades cleared off the bug guts. This was the joy of driving across the southern United States.

But tonight, DJ was going home. Home seemed like something she should look forward to, but she was not certain if joy was the emotion she was feeling at this moment. She was simply tired. They'd run into bad weather. Tropical storm-strength winds and tons of rain exhausted her. Her arms and back ached from driving the big pickup truck. Yawning, she reached toward the cup holder for more coffee. Just a few more miles. We're almost home.

The interstate's exit number arrived at last. DJ clutched and downshifted. Her speed dropped to thirty-five miles per hour. She cranked the steering wheel into a gentle right-handed curve onto the slope of the exit ramp. Then she merged with traffic on the highway. She was heading north and following the green road signs toward Foggy Creek, Texas. Homeward bound.

DJ loved her father, Dale, very much. They shared a strong bond and were similar in many ways. He had taught her to drive the truck when she was fifteen and had a learner's permit. She had her license now, and she loved helping her dad visit other ranches, drive to livestock auctions, and haul cattle.

DJ's mother, Maude, liked the quiet, scenic beauty of Foggy Creek and their family ranch. She always said she didn't like to haul cattle all over Texas. She was a homebody, through and through.

Three and a half years ago, when DJ was in ninth grade, her dad had a heart attack. After that, they decided to homeschool her. This way, someone could be with her dad round the clock as he recovered, and someone could tend to the ranch. She and her mom took turns. When one was feeding the cattle or mending fences, the other stayed with her dad. It worked out pretty well. DJ thrived in homeschool, so they just kept it up.

Although DJ missed out on a more common high school experience, she didn't regret it. She loved the ranch, she loved hauling cattle, and she loved imagining a world filled with adventures and interesting things. She did miss her friends from town. But everyone in her family worked hard to maintain the ranch, including her. It was always a struggle to make money and pay the bills. But she felt pride in contributing to her family's business.

DJ didn't shy away from big dreams. She wanted an Ivy League college education where she could learn about how to run a business and make lots of money. Then, she could turn the ranch into a big-time operation and her family could live in style without worrying about scraping by.

As soon as the engine stopped, Dad jumped out of the truck. DJ was right behind him. They were finally home! The faded white farmhouse sat at an angle on the short foundation of stone and cinder blocks. The porch, with peeling white paint and pillars, hid in deep shadows cast by the yard lights near the gates. The tar paper shingles needed replacement in several spots. Yet this modest home had been in the family for four generations. Now it was home for DJ, her mom and dad, and her mom's brother, Clive.

DJ's Uncle Clive had moved in with the

family last year when he got out of the Army. Uncle Clive helped around the ranch and raised hunting hounds. Each litter brought in a small amount of cash. But payments were always due: property taxes, second mortgage payments, and loan payments on the tractors and farm equipment. They did not have a life of luxury.

A kitchen table light shined in the window. DJ knew her mom had been waiting up for them. Her mom always worried when they were on the road.

The front door swung open and DJ's mom came running out of the house.

"I missed you so much!" she said as she squeezed each of them tightly.

With an eye roll, DJ said, "It was only five days, Mom." She let her mom give her a peck on the cheek and answered, "But I missed you too."

After giving each other hugs, her mom said, "Come inside. There's a lot to catch you two up on."

They all sat at the kitchen table.

"Some strange things have been happening in the past couple of days," Mom said.

"What do you mean? What strange things?" DJ asked.

"There are big black Suburbans parked all over town. Men in dark business suits are walking through the woods. And I keep seeing weird lights at night." Mom spoke with a tremor in her voice.

"Did Clive go out and take a look?" Dad asked.

"He did. Couldn't find anything out of the ordinary. Though his dogs have been acting mighty flighty lately." Mom drummed her fingers on the table. "Howling at odd hours of the night. Like something's creeping around the kennels. Makes me nervous."

"Well, that can't be good," DJ said. "Want me to go out tomorrow morning? Take a look?"

Mom nodded. "But be careful."

"I will. Nothing will happen in broad daylight, anyhow."

DJ yawned. She felt too tired to give it much more worry. It could wait until the morning. Anyway, the men in black suits had to be the feds. She was sure they could handle things.

"I'm going to my room," DJ said to her parents. "Talk more in the morning. Night. Love you."

After DJ went into her bedroom, she decided to send a quick text to her best friend, Consuela. Even if it was two in the morning.

DJ: I'm home!!!!

She set down her phone and was surprised to hear it buzz a minute later. She assumed Consuela would be sleeping.

Consuela: Hola, girl

Before DJ had time to say anything, Consuela sent another message.

Consuela: The girls want to SEE you, you know. It's been a few weeks!

DJ felt bad she hadn't been spending more time with her friends. Lately, her family had been extra busy with the farm and planning her and her dad's trips to other cattle ranches. And when DJ wasn't working on her family's farm, she was doing homework.

DJ: I know! Same. Let's meet at the diner tomorrow.

Consuela: Okay, I gotta get some sleep. Later.

DJ: Night!

DJ put the phone on her dresser. Smiling, she thought about seeing Consuela at the diner and chatting with her about the new steers her dad planned to purchase. Consuela loved all things agricultural, just like DJ. But first, she needed to get some sleep. With a yawn, DJ nestled into her quilt and fell asleep.

The next morning, DJ dragged herself out of bed. Her mom had set the timer on the coffee pot so it would be ready at dawn. She was always looking out for them. DJ helped herself to a cup. As she sat in the kitchen, she noticed the home's decor seemed to consist of bad-smelling baits and traps filled with dead insects. Pest removal must have been on Uncle Clive's list of chores. Yuck. There was a load of dead flies stuck on the fly strips.

She walked out of the house through the back screen door. The pickup truck was covered in dew. She walked in bare feet, careful to avoid the droppings of their hound dogs. Then she gave thanks for the beautiful day. This remained from her childhood Sunday school training. Always be thankful, no matter what.

DJ enjoyed the cool of the early morning

and the sunrise. The day was open to new possibilities. The songbirds fluttered around the bird feeders. The ranch was quiet and peaceful. No tractors rumbled. No dogs barked. The world was still sleeping. Though it would be time to feed the cattle soon.

While looking around, she saw an odd circle of blue plastic flags hanging on a wire fence. It was just past their property line. The flags were strange, but it was the huge sinkhole that really caught her attention. Downhill from the house, near the trees, the sagebrush was uprooted. Thick pieces of brown mud were visible. DJ wondered if this meant new construction. Was somebody building a fancy housing development out here next to their ranch? Or building a human-made lake? She knew that the land was private property. Who knows what the owners were up to?

DJ walked back toward her house. Her stomach growled. She needed breakfast. As she went inside, she heard her parents' bedroom door open. Someone was awake. The light flicked on in the bathroom.

"Mom?" DJ asked, standing outside of the bathroom. A flush from the toilet was the reply. "Want some toast?"

"Um-hmmm," mumbled her mom.

DJ went to the refrigerator to find food. A few moments later, her mom came into the kitchen.

"Where's Dad?" DJ asked.

"Still in bed, honey." Her mom rubbed her eyes and poured herself a cup of coffee. "Why are you up so early? You need your rest. You could have slept in since it's Saturday."

DJ shrugged. "Just glad to be home, I guess."

She put some bread in the toaster and took the peanut butter from the cupboard. Time to eat. She made a plate for herself and for her mom. Then she looked out of the window and saw those blue flags fluttering in the wind. DJ decided to ask her mom some questions to clear this up. She set the plates of peanut butter toast on the kitchen table.

"Have you had anyone out on the property? Are you having any work done?"

Her mom plopped heavily into a kitchen chair. "Honey, what are you talking about?"

"The big hole just past our fence line. The blue flags. Didn't you see them?"

"The new owners must have been doing some work out there." She shrugged. "I've been busy. Ain't got time to watch the neighbors much. Although those guys I told you about last night, the ones in the Suburbans, they've been poking around."

"Hmm, I wonder what's going on."

DJ finished eating her peanut butter toast. She chugged down one more cup of coffee. Then she decided it was time for her to look around. She got dressed in her flannel shirt, jeans, and boots. Then she went off to the strand of trees past their property line.

Glancing back into the clearing toward her house, she looked at the rusted tractor. It stood as a landmark, unmoving for a long time. It was her grandfather's tractor. Then she saw Uncle Clive come out of the house. Time to feed his hounds. DJ could hear the dogs howling for their breakfast.

DJ kept wandering closer to the sinkhole. She went through the cluster of trees.

Mesquite and juniper pines make for sparer forests. They are thick with underbrush and thorns. Ducking under branches, she headed uphill. Most of this Texas countryside was flat, but there were some low rises.

As an angry and sad child, DJ used to come out here to avoid the family troubles, often about money and bills, and to watch the jackrabbits scamper around. She knew this land better than she knew her own mother, and that was saying a lot. DJ was wandering partly from memory and some weird curious feeling that was pulling her toward the sinkhole.

A stench hit her as soon as she crested an embankment. Her gag reflex kicked in. It smelled putrid. Hovering in a cloud about five feet away from her was a swarm of black flies. A dead dog. She gagged and felt like she was going to throw up. The swarming flies landed and took off in near-endless loops over the dog's body. DJ put her hands over her mouth and went closer. *Whose dog was it,* she thought. There weren't any neighbors for miles.

Patches! It was her uncle's hound, Patches.

No. No. No. No. Patches! She covered her mouth and ran back to her house.

She stumbled through the front door. Her mom and dad were sitting at the kitchen table.

"What happened to you?" Mom asked.

DJ mumbled, "I don't know."

Her dad rushed toward her. "Maude, look at her! She looks awful."

"Come lay down," her mom said.

They led DJ to the sofa in the living room. Her mom brought her a quilt and covered her. Then she took her temperature. DJ had a fever and a bloody nose.

"What brought this on?" she asked.

DJ stammered out, "Dead, dead dog."

Her father gently applied a cold washcloth to her forehead. This was the cure that seemed to work for just about any ailment. He looked concerned and offered comforting words. "What did you get into?" he asked.

DJ wiped her nose. "I, um, I don't know. I headed to the property line to see the big hole with the blue flags around it." She stopped and took a labored breath. "But then I found

Patches. Dead." She started to sob. "There were flies all over his body. Huge swarms of 'em. Ain't like anything I've seen before."

Her dad leaned over and hugged her. "Oh, no, DJ."

"He looked terrible. Like he died in some kind of fight." She sobbed. "He was a good boy."

"I'll tell Uncle Clive. He'll go get Patches and bring him home for a proper burial."

She sniffled and blew her nose on a tissue. "Okay."

"Honey, lie down for a spell," Mom said. "Seeing Patches must have shocked you."

"Mom, Dad, something is weird. I have to get to the bottom of this. It didn't look right."

"I know, honey. We'll figure it out. Together." Mom rubbed DJ's shoulder to comfort her, "But, first, have some soup."

A few minutes later, her mom came back into the living room with a bowl of chicken noodle soup, hot from the microwave.

"Mom, what do you think killed Patches?"

"It's hard to say. Do you think a coyote got him?"

"I don't know. I didn't look that closely. The flies were everywhere."

Mom sighed. "I'm going to call the utility company. See who has been out there. And if they ran over a dog on accident or saw anything weird." She went into the kitchen to make the call on the landline.

After ten minutes, her mom began talking to a person on the other end of the line. DJ could hear only her mom's half of the conversation. It wasn't much. A couple of no sirs and a thank you.

Her mom came back to the living room. "The utility company hasn't been out there. It's not their project or sinkhole. They hadn't heard of anyone's dog gone missing or dead either."

"Who in the world is out there, then, working?" Dad asked.

Mom shrugged. "Could be anyone, I reckon."

DJ watched her dad as he paced their small living room. "If it isn't our utility company, then who owns the land? Who is at work?" He scratched his head. "The government. It's the government to blame. Those feds hanging around town. Probably building some top-secret research facility."

"Oh, stop it," her mom said. "No more conspiracy theories. No more blaming the government. The dog is dead. DJ is a mess. Let's worry about her and mind our own business."

"I'll be fine," DJ said. "I'm meeting up with Consuela today."

Mom shook her head. "Sorry, honey, but you can't today. You need to rest and get better. Consuela will understand."

DJ thought about arguing but knew it was no use. Once her mom made a decision, it was final.

By the next morning, DJ's fever had gone down. She felt a little better. Although she couldn't watch when Uncle Clive brought Patches back to their house to bury him. It was too much. She stayed in her room and cried.

When she got herself under control, she texted Consuela.

> DJ: Sorry about canceling yesterday. Want to have breakfast at the diner? I need to talk to you

Consuela responded quickly.

Consuela: Sure! See you in an hour?

DJ: C U there

DJ borrowed Uncle Clive's truck and headed into Foggy Creek. As she drove, she heard powerful helicopter blades. She saw them zoom over her. They were heading toward the county line. They looked like military helicopters, Black Hawks, but there were no emblems or markings on the helicopters. *Something is up*, she thought. *We never see these around here. There's no base for hundreds of miles.* She pulled over and texted her dad.

DJ: Two Black Hawks heading to the County Line. No markings.

Dad: Where are you?

DJ: Heading into town. I'm on the side of the road.

Dad: Let me ask Stan if he's heard anything.

Stan was her dad's Army friend. They'd known each other for years. If anyone would know what was going on, he would.

DJ: Okay

Dad: Drive safely. No texting and driving.

Consuela was already at the diner and had ordered two heaping plates of bacon and eggs. DJ rushed in and slid into the booth.

"I missed you," Consuela said as she squeezed DJ's hands. "You look like the living dead, though, no offense."

DJ brushed the hair out of her eyes. "Yeah, we've been on the road way too much."

Consuela shook her head. "No. This isn't

your usual road-weary look. You look pasty. Have you seen a ghost?"

DJ started to tell Consuela about Patches, but then she saw two men in black suits walk into the diner. She lifted her chin, signaling to Consuela to take notice of who came in. Consuela raised an eyebrow. Not your typical clientele in Foggy Creek.

The men took the booth right behind theirs. Consuela and DJ pretended to pay no attention to the men, but they both stopped talking and focused all their energy on slowly eating their eggs—very slowly—and eavesdropping on the men behind them.

"They just told me to return to base," one of the men in a black suit said. "It's not right. Something is off. I can feel it."

The man he was with said, "What is your malfunction? Do what you are told. You are a sworn officer. This is not your problem. How do you imagine this working out in your favor?"

"Ok. Gee, relax. I won't do anything stupid, but you know that isn't right."

"Could be immigration, DEA, heck, CIA for all we know. Leave it alone. Follow your superior's orders."

DJ squirmed in her seat. It was the feds. And whatever was going down sure sounded like it was top-secret.

Then the server came up, interrupted the conversation, and offered the men more coffee. That was the end of that. DJ could only wonder if the two men had anything to do with the Black Hawks or with the huge sinkhole out by her house. Or if that was another government agency like the Marines or the FBI?

Consuela leaned across the table. "What's going on? You are on edge, girl. Snap out of it. Stop daydreaming."

"Eat up. I'll tell you outside. After you have time to digest your food."

After they finished, DJ and Consuela went to the park to hang out by the fountain. DJ told her about Patches, the flies, the sinkhole, the Suburbans and men in dark suits, and the helicopters. Then she recapped the fragmented conversation they'd overheard while they were having breakfast. "It's all creepy," she concluded.

Consuela was quiet. Then she looked past DJ and said, "Hey, isn't that your dad heading into the diner?"

DJ turned around. Sure enough it was her dad. He didn't usually eat breakfast this late or in town. He preferred the farm fresh eggs at their place.

"I'm going to see what's up, okay?"

"No problem. I've got to get to work soon anyway. See you later, DJ!"

DJ sprinted across the street and went right back into the diner.

Her dad was seated at a booth with Sergeant Mark, a police officer and a longtime friend of the family. DJ walked up to them.

"DJ!" Dad said. "What are you doing?"

Before she could answer, Sergeant Mark chimed in. "Nice ax-wielding barbarian on your T-shirt. And compliments on the flannel shirt. Very cool," Sergeant Mark added with a smile. "You look like a person from our era.

Right, Dale? Remember? Seattle Grunge and Kris Cobos?"

DJ had known Sergeant Mark since she was a baby. He was practically like another uncle to her. He appreciated her "quirkiness," as Consuela called it.

"Sit with us," her dad said, patting the bench beside him. "We were going to talk about that new construction site out by our place."

He was not wasting any time. "Don't utilities need permission to go on your land, digging stuff up?"

"What are you talking about?" Sergeant Mark asked.

But DJ's dad didn't stop to answer; he just asked more questions. "Wouldn't they need to notify a homeowner if they needed to work on your property or cross through it? Because somebody has been on our property. No doubt about it. They're causing damage. Would the government tell you if they were looking for something on your land?"

Sergeant Mark looked dazed and very

confused. “What are we talking about? Trespassing? Or a government conspiracy?”

Dad took a sip from his mug and sat back frustrated, “Why am I wasting my time with you, Mark? You are clueless. Keep up with me, okay?”

“Hold on a minute, Dale. Give me a break. You invited me to coffee, to talk. Not to go all loopy. Besides, I’ve seen some crazy stuff around here lately, too, if you’d give me two seconds to tell you. Stop rattling on, man.”

DJ’s ears pricked up. “What have you seen?”

Mark said, “Oh, I don’t know, maybe eight Black Hawks flying east of town . . . in the middle of the night . . . for no apparent reason.”

“Really? Tell me more,” DJ said. More Black Hawks than the ones she saw. Things were getting very interesting.

Mark folded his hands over the menu. “What’s to tell? Dispatch tells me to return to the station and get clear of the area, which makes NO sense. Then I called Stan to see if he’s heard anything from his military buddies.

He was no help. If he has heard anything, he won't tell me."

"What are you babbling about? Does Stan know something and he isn't talking?" Her dad was getting impatient.

Shrugging, Sergeant Mark said, "I wish I knew." He lowered his voice. "Don't look now, but three gruesome feds just pulled in the parking lot. And I think they just ran your plates."

DJ turned and saw the men in black. They were not the same ones that she and Consuela saw earlier. But they were more feds. No doubt about it. *What in the world was going on in sleepy little old Foggy Creek, Texas*, DJ wondered.

The government agents strode into the diner, heading to a table in the back corner. They wore their sunglasses inside. DJ thought they looked pretty boss. They were more confident than the last bunch. *Must be the senior officers*, she thought.

When the server came to them and asked for their order, they quickly—and efficiently—ordered. No time for small talk. After the server walked away, they pretended to ignore their surroundings. The other customers tried not to stare at them. *How bizarre*, DJ thought. The normally noisy diner became quiet as a library. No one was chatting. Folks seemed on edge with the federal agents in the place.

Half an hour later, after the feds left the diner, DJ told Mark about the weirder parts of what she had seen since coming home. They concluded that helicopters landing in the middle of nowhere at night was interesting but could be explained. Maybe. Like maybe it was a military practice drill. That could be a possibility. A dead dog and an unexplained sinkhole near your property were odd. However, these did not guarantee supernatural events. Dogs die all the time. It did not signal a government conspiracy. Maybe the feds were after some criminals. Who knew?

Dr. Perez did not want to be in Foggy Creek, Texas. He was a world-renowned scientist from Boston. He hated leaving his work behind at the university and did not trust others to hold his lectures in his absence. This trip to middle-of-nowhere Texas was a waste of his time. *I have better things to do*, he thought. *Sinkholes, of all things. That's such a basic geological occurrence. Nothing extraordinary and certainly nothing that would generate money, not like fracking surveys for the oil companies. Although*, he told himself, *the grant money from this project would be nice.*

The government had contacted him and offered him a rather large sum of grant money to come all the way out here and take soil samples. They said the grant money was so large because they needed these samples right away. A little extra pay to sweeten the deal. He simply had to get some local Texas graduate students in the field so they could do the dirty work of collecting samples and taking measurements. Then they'd get to the bottom of these recent sinkholes.

Yet, Dr. Perez found no local graduate students willing to do the fieldwork. Mainly because there wasn't a college within a two-hundred-mile radius of Foggy Creek. So, here he was, pushing blue flags into the mud around these pits. They were markers of where he had drawn soil samples. Now he was dripping in sweat and cursing his luck. Could it get any hotter in Texas? What he wouldn't give to be back in his air-conditioned office in Boston.

Grim, sad thoughts troubled DJ's mind. Lost in her throbbing pain of the worst headache ever, she lay in her dark bedroom. Thoughts darted around in her mind. Foggy Creek seemed like a typical cow town. A few small businesses, a park, a hospital, lots of cows, and open land for miles. Not much, compared to the big bright cities of Houston or Austin. Foggy Creek literally rolled up its sidewalks at five o'clock. There was no nightlife, nothing. Usually. But here she was, puzzling over the strange details, trying to piece them together to make sense of it all. *Why would federal agents be swarming Foggy Creek? Ugh.* Her head hurt so bad. She felt sick to her stomach. Maybe she had gotten food poisoning from one of their stops on the road. She'd never felt so awful in her entire life.

"Dad!" she called out. "Dad! Bring me a bowl!"

He rushed into her bedroom, just in time, with a large plastic bowl. DJ leaned over and threw up in it.

"DJ, we need to get you to a doctor. You're getting worse, not better."

At the clinic, DJ stood in the corner, waiting for the nurse to call her name. Her father paced in the room. The clinic was short-staffed. A dozen people were waiting to see the doctor. Many of them were coughing or had bloody noses. It was taking too long, and she felt miserable with a headache that would not go away.

Finally, after an hour, it was her turn. The nurse led her back to the exam room. She took her vitals.

Then Dr. Patel came in and examined her. "Everything seems within the normal range," she told DJ.

"But why is my head throbbing?"

"Maybe a migraine. Some women get them now and then. Might be hormonal."

DJ shook her head. "Not me. I never get them." She pulled the hospital gown tighter over herself. She felt cold. "Can you do an x-ray, an MRI? Something?" She knew her body and something was not right.

"We can run some blood work. Maybe you are anemic. You could have low iron, low blood sugar levels, or you may be dehydrated. We'll see. But it will take about three days to get the results." Dr. Patel got the vials and needles out of a drawer. "Ready?"

DJ nodded. Dr. Patel found a vein and filled purple topped vials with blood for lab work. DJ turned her head away and didn't watch. She couldn't stand the sight of blood.

When DJ came out of the exam room, she saw her dad sitting in the jam-packed waiting room. There were at least forty people there now, moaning and groaning. A few looked feverish. Others were shivering. A couple had bloody noses. A little boy was vomiting in a paper bag. Disgusting. But the symptoms were the same as hers.

"It must be going around," her dad said. "Looks just like what you've been having."

It isn't flu season, DJ thought. She hoped the lab results would get done fast. *What did I catch?*

After they drove home, DJ got a weird call from Consuela.

"DJ! My mom said half the town has been to the pharmacy. Everyone's buying up fever-reducing medicines. And cold and flu meds."

Consuela's mom had worked at the pharmacy since the girls started kindergarten, so she'd heard and seen everything. She also knew everyone in town by their first name.

DJ paced around her bedroom. "What's wrong with them?"

"Don't know. They seem to be trying just about anything to ease their symptoms." Consuela paused for a moment, then added, "My mom said they all looked like death."

Shivers ran up and down DJ's spine.

An hour later, DJ was sitting with her uncle and her parents at their kitchen table. Uncle Clive looked tired and worn down.

"Dr. Skinner came out to look at the dogs," he said. "It wasn't good news."

DJ loved all of Uncle Clive's dogs. She hoped more of them wouldn't die. "What's going on?"

"All the dogs are very sick. She thinks most of them aren't going to make it." Uncle Clive paused before continuing. "It's not just us. She said her clinic's been slammed with calls. Pets and livestock all over town are dropping dead."

"I'm so sorry about the dogs, Clive," Mom said. "We will do everything we can to help."

When Uncle Clive spoke next, he was quiet and his voice was shaky. "Dr. Skinner said she's been making ranch calls all over the county. At Delgado's Ranch, she said the longhorns were distressed."

"And that means what?" DJ asked.

"They had bloody noses. Dr. Skinner said it's quite unusual. All the animal illnesses have been unusual. She's been running tests and sent some samples to the University of Texas, but she is still waiting on lab results."

DJ's breath caught in her throat. If Mr. Delgado's longhorns were getting sick and dying, would their herd catch it too?

"How are our cows?" DJ asked.

"Okay, so far." Uncle Clive sighed. "Only the dogs are sick for now."

"Until we know what's going on, we shouldn't bring any new bulls onto our ranch," Dad said. "We can't risk getting a sick animal that will infect the healthy ones."

DJ's phone pinged with messages from

Consuela. She had heard about all the animals in town getting sick. DJ remembered cases of bird flu from a few years ago, yet this virus—or whatever it was—did not quite present like that. *What was going on*, DJ wondered for what felt like the hundredth time.

The next evening, DJ's family found Uncle Clive covered in dog blood and vomiting loudly into the toilet. He wretched so violently that his aim missed the toilet.

"Get it into the toilet," DJ said angrily. She was too miserable to have much empathy. She still felt like garbage and her migraine was not going away.

He looked up at her. His eyes looked distant, cloudy.

"Oh no," her mom said as she came into the vomit-covered bathroom. "Clive, let me help you up and clean you off. Just a sec though. Let me get the mess off the floor. Stay put."

Uncle Clive's boney frame was covered in sweat. He shivered between dry heaves as DJ's mom got the mop and bucket.

Then she got Clive to his feet. "How does this feel?" she asked as she wiped his face with a cold washcloth.

"Better," he said in a weak whisper.

"You need to lie down. Rest." She led Clive upstairs to his bedroom.

DJ found her favorite quilt and went to lay down on the sofa.

"Can you turn off the TV, Dad?"

"Why, sweetie? Don't you want to watch a movie with me?"

"The light from the TV makes my head hurt worse."

Her mom came back down the stairs.

"Dale, Clive ain't looking good. We should take him to the clinic."

"It's the same thing that DJ got. And they didn't do anything to help her there." He coughed, took a sip of iced tea. "Besides trips to the doctor cost a lot of money."

Her mom grunted. "You stubborn old man," she said. "But what if we catch it?"

"I don't know. Can't afford for all of us to go to the doctor."

"I ain't taking chances. I'm heading into town to pick up some latex gloves and surgical masks. Keep us from getting it."

When DJ's mom came home with masks and gloves, she said, "Here, Dale. If you get close to DJ or Clive, put it on. Just like nurses in operating rooms do."

Both of DJ's parents put on surgical masks, which made her feel strange and a little paranoid. They'd never done anything like this before.

DJ's only highlight of the past few days was the long talk she had with Consuela the night before. They often joked their video chats were what kept them sane. Except this video chat was not as fun or as normal. They had a lot of information to share about the mysterious events in town. A bunch of men-in-black government types were staying at the motel. They ate every meal together in the diner. All the locals knew it was weird and the government-types all ignored the stares. The men wore blank, grim faces, sunglasses, and earpieces. They drove a small fleet of heavy, black Suburbans, definitely the Hollywood codebook for government agents.

DJ told Consuela that they had gone into town for some medical answers at the clinic a few days ago. This migraine, or whatever it was, was horrible. And they didn't have any answers.

But Consuela had really lost it about the pets and livestock. "Not just sick people. It's animals too. Cows. Dogs. They're all sick or dead!" Consuela paused. "Thirteen more sinkholes have opened up around the outskirts of town. Thirteen!"

"No way," DJ said. "All like the one by my house?"

"Almost exactly like it. And, get this, there's some big-time scientist named Dr. Perez here investigating them."

"It's like what you see on those supernatural TV shows."

"And we're living in it," Consuela added.

That did not make DJ feel any better.

Over the next couple of days, DJ stayed

home and nursed her flu symptoms, or at least what she thought were flu symptoms. Consuela brought her things like chicken soup and sci-fi novels. But she was careful, staying on the porch, never coming inside the house. She also wore a mask. She told DJ that more people and animals had gotten sick. So many, in fact, that the military had set up an emergency hospital in the parking lot of the high school. Rumors of quarantine, or a lockdown, were starting to spread.

DJ woke up around three o'clock. Her bed was soaked in sweat and her sheets were a mess. Her dreams had been troubled, almost a vision of something to come. She felt hot and clammy.

She took an aspirin. *When was this virus going to clear her system*, she wondered. Then she showered and put on fresh pajamas. She thought about going back to bed, but then she heard a noise coming from the kitchen.

Her dad was rummaging through the refrigerator.

"Morning," she said as she walked up to him and hugged him.

"Couldn't sleep?"

She shook her head.

"Me neither. All these sick cows have gotten to me. Can't stop worrying about it."

Her dad's phone rang, breaking the early morning silence.

"Hello? Mark?" he asked.

Sergeant Mark? At this hour? *Uh-oh*, she thought, *nothing good can come from a cop call at 4:30 in the morning.*

Her dad muttered out a couple of uh-huhs and then added, "Mark, I'm going to put you on speaker phone, okay? So DJ can hear you too."

"I feel like dirt. Like I got food poisoning," Mark said.

"Like DJ's symptoms?"

"Yeah."

"Are you going to the doc?" Dad asked.

"I already went. Man, am I tired."

"Don't push yourself. Your body needs to rest. What is it? Do they know yet?"

"Don't know. Doc thinks it might be some kind of new virus or flu. It is nasty." Mark coughed, then he said, "When I was on patrol tonight, I noticed how oddly quiet things had gotten. Usually, I see a few stray dogs roaming around the dumpsters. Not a one tonight. So I drove toward the high school. I can usually count on kids hanging around, listening to loud rap music. But instead of kids, there were lines of cars. People were waiting to get checked at the Army hospital. I got stuck there directing traffic for three hours. Then I had to finish my patrol over by the stockyards, west of the school." Mark gagged.

DJ cringed. He didn't sound good at all.

"When I got to the stockyard, I rolled down my window. I didn't hear any steers grunting or bellowing. So I scanned the fence line and didn't see any signs of cattle. I decided to park the patrol car next to the fence and get out. When I got to the fence, I turned on my flashlight, looked over the fence, and threw up. There, no more than ten feet in front of me, was a pile of dead cows. Black flies swarmed over the carcasses. I staggered backward, holding back more vomit. I made it back to my car and raced back to the police station. I notified my boss and filed a report. Then I called you."

"Oh, no!" DJ gasped. "Did the dead cows have ooze coming out of their nostrils?"

"Yes. How did you know?" Mark asked. "Is that what your dead dog looked like? Was there blood and ooze everywhere?"

DJ said, "Exactly."

"We got a big problem on our hands. I don't know what it is, but it isn't normal or natural. I'm calling Dr. Skinner."

With that, Mark hung up.

"Dad, what is going on?" After Mark's call, DJ was even more nervous than before. "Is it Cowpox? Mad Cow disease? What?"

"Sweetheart, we don't know. But I sure hope Dr. Skinner finds out soon."

A few minutes later, Dad's phone pinged again with a new text message. "It's Mark," he said, reading the message and then passing DJ the phone.

Mark: She saw the same thing out at the Martinez and the Delgado ranches. Not sure what's happening yet. Waiting for lab work that she sent off to the university.

Even though Dr. Perez was a world-famous scientist, he struggled to keep his students' attention and interest, especially in video conference classes. The topic for this virtual lecture was sinkholes. Not as exciting as an earthquake, but maybe just as damaging.

"Who did the reading last night?" he asked the sea of faces on the laptop screen.

"I read that sinkholes are holes in the ground," one student answered as others chuckled.

"How brilliant of you. Let's talk about

the causes of sinkholes," Dr. Perez continued. "Then we'll talk about my exciting trip to rural Texas for the best explanation. Time for field experience."

Since he first came to Foggy Creek a week ago, thirteen additional sinkholes had appeared. *Things are becoming unusual*, he thought. *Strange, even for a weird little town, just a dot on the map, in Texas.* He really did need his students to take this seriously. Most importantly, he needed them in the field, collecting data and samples.

"Who is willing to hop on a plane and head to Texas?" he asked the virtual class. "The grant will cover your airfare, food, and lodging. Plus, you'll get a $200 paycheck."

Three students raised their hands.

"Good, thank you," he said. "We will chat after class. But first, let's review sinkholes and composition." He flipped the slide on his presentation. "Freshwater is trapped between the grains of sand. People pump that water out. The groundwater is often recharged by rain. But people can pump the water out faster than the rain can replace it. The water might take a long time to move down into the aquifer."

A few students turned their cameras off. *Virtual lectures*, he thought, *are not my strong point.* But he carried on. "Sinkholes could also result from pumping oil out of the ground. The oil could be worth a lot of money, and many companies were interested in finding supplies in the US. Hydraulic fracturing or fracking uses water, sand, and additives to break rocks and extract oil and natural gas," he explained.

Then he flipped to the next slide on his virtual presentation. "Sinkholes are also prevalent because, when underground oil reservoirs are being emptied, the overburden is left unsupported and the land collapses. That is why environmental impact studies are a thing of necessity. So, either a lack of water or oil is causing the sinkholes outside of Foggy Creek. It is the only possible explanation. But I need students to help gather samples to be sure."

After he wrapped up his virtual class,

he met with the three students who were interested in the fieldwork in Foggy Creek. He told them more about their upcoming work and about the strange microscopic cells that could live in the sinkholes. Cells need water. Where there is water, you can find life, after all. He wanted his students to get him some field samples from around the sinkholes. They would run tests in Texas and send a second set to his colleagues in Mexico for replication and confirmation. They would get down to the root cause of all these sinkholes.

"The days will be long and hot, but you will get valuable scientific experience," he told the three young men. "Pack hiking boots, sunscreen, bug spray, a hat, and other appropriate clothing. Have my assistant book your flights. Her office is number 1313, next door to my office. Got it?"

He saw three bobbing heads on his laptop screen. "Very good, gentlemen. I'll see you soon in beautiful Foggy Creek, Texas. Safe travels."

Then he clicked the end meeting button and shut down the virtual class. Now, time to get back out to that sinkhole near the sorghum fields. It looked like it was growing every day.

DJ was sleepy again. She was having trouble keeping track of time, the passing of days and nights. Lately, she couldn't focus or stay awake. But it was the weird visions that really bothered her. She thought she saw aliens. It would happen randomly and out of the blue. Like when she was outside, sitting on the porch, she thought she saw a grayish figure run by the truck. Or when she went to the mailbox at the end of the lane, she thought one was running across the field.

She shook her head and rubbed her eyes.

That was the stuff from the sci-fi novels she loved, not reality. She felt her forehead. *Maybe she was feverish and that was what was causing all this*, she told herself. *Why hadn't the lab results given them any information? Everything came back "within normal range." Something certainly was not "normal."*

DJ got out of bed and went to the kitchen for some water. Through the window, she could see her dad. He was outside working on his pickup truck. He'd washed the truck and vacuumed the interior to get it nice and ready for the next haul. He hated a dirty truck.

The wind picked up, and DJ noticed the rattling wind chimes that hung from their front porch. Her head throbbed. The wind chimes did not help her headache. She felt dizzy. The wind howled, louder and louder. Instead of dying down, the wind picked up strength.

"What the?" DJ looked up at the blue sky. "Tornado?" she said out loud. She started to scream at her dad, to get his attention and warn him to take cover, but instead of a tornado she saw an enormous disk-shaped ship, or plane, she didn't know—UFO—zoom over their house.

The spaceship hovered over her dad. It lowered.

She saw her dad raise his hands and clutch his forehead like he was in pain. Blood dripped down onto his white T-shirt. She heard him yell, "Get out of here! Leave me alone!" A beam of white light shown down on him. He dropped to the ground, unconscious.

Before she could rush to her dad, she heard her mom's screams.

"DJ! Call 9-1-1! Quick!"

She rushed to her mom, who was standing in Uncle Clive's room.

"He's not responsive. Call the paramedics! Quick!"

Uncle Clive was on his bed. He wouldn't wake up. DJ grabbed her cell phone and called the ambulance.

At the hospital, Uncle Clive and her dad remained in stable condition. But they were both in comas. DJ's mom sat at her dad's bedside, holding his hand, while DJ sat next to Uncle Clive's hospital bed.

"What happened, Mom?"

"I don't know. Clive's fever had spiked, so he went to lay down. I went upstairs to check on him." She fought back tears. "And he was like, like this."

DJ bit down on her lower lip, struggling to make sense of what she saw. Did she truly see an alien spaceship strike her father down? Or was this virus making her delusional, causing her to see things that were not really there? What about Uncle Clive?

"Are they going to die?"

Her mom didn't answer. She wiped a tear from her eye.

"When will the doctor get here?" DJ asked.

"I don't know, honey. They're dealing with sick people everywhere. People are lined up in gurneys. All the rooms are full." Her voice trailed off. A drop of blood trickled from her nose. Suddenly, her mom slumped over in her chair.

"Mom! Mom! I don't feel so good," DJ said before she crumpled to the floor. Only half awake, DJ felt her phone buzz. She took it out and saw one message.

Consuela: My mom's sick. Took her to her doctor's office. It's packed. EVERYBODY is sick.

Then DJ's world went dark.

Three bored college students from Boston were working around a muddy sinkhole. Jake, Steve, and Juan were all geology majors. They had signed up to investigate the sinkholes in Foggy Creek for Dr. Perez as a career-building move and as a way to earn brownie points with the tough geology professor. Now, standing in the mud and the sweltering heat, they were not too sure how happy they were about that decision.

"I am tired of this," Steve said. "It is hotter than Hades and there is no nightlife in this town."

"All you do is complain," Jake said.

Juan, trying to get them to focus and work, said, "Guys, none of this will get our samples collected any faster."

"How long have we been in this hole?" Steve asked. "I'm starving."

"Too long," Jake said.

They were sweaty and thirsty. Juan wondered if fieldwork was still a valuable experience these days. *Would he land a sweet job after college?* He pushed his doubts deep down inside himself. *Focus on the samples*, he told himself. *Pay attention.* Collection rules for sterile samples were strict. Careless mistakes cost time and money. They had been repeatedly reminded of that by their university supervisors. Plastic vials and bottles were carefully dated, labeled, and stored in coolers of dry ice. Mists of carbon dioxide greeted each deposit. There was no room for error. Juan went slowly, accurately, and safely.

Jake's grating voice jolted Juan out of his thoughts. "Why on Earth are we shipping these samples to some school in Mexico?"

"Because Dr. Perez is running this project, not you. And that's what he said he wants." Juan wiped his face with his bandana. Dust hung in the air from all the shoveling they had done. Juan closed the last case that held the samples. "All done for the day. Finally. Let's meet Dr. Perez at the diner. We can give him the samples and get a sandwich." Juan tried to clear the weird tickle at the back of his throat.

"Man, my eyes burn," Steve said. "Been out here in the heat too long."

"My eyes are so dry that my contact lenses are stuck to my eyeballs," Jake said.

Juan cleared his throat again. "Come on. We need to rehydrate and get some food. Then we'll feel better."

His lips started to feel itchy. Weird. But he had never been in such a dry climate before, so maybe this was typical. He loaded the cases into the truck, and they headed into Foggy Creek.

As Juan drove the truck down the highway, he got a throbbing headache. "Oh! Man!" he cried out, veering off the road.

The truck crashed into a boulder. Steve and Jake flew forward, their faces almost slamming into the windshield.

When the truck stopped, Steve yelled, "Why'd you do a thing like that? You could've killed us!"

Juan dropped his head onto the steering wheel. "My head is pounding." Then he vomited all over himself.

"Get out of the truck, dude! Gross!" Jake shouted, opening the passenger's door and jumping out. He went around to the driver's side and pulled Juan out. "Go puke next to that boulder."

Stumbling around, clutching his stomach, Juan retched again. His knees buckled and he was on the ground.

"Holy Hannah! My stomach!" Jake yelled before a throbbing pain doubled him over.

Steve ran to Jake. He tried to roll him over. "Jake! Jake!" Turning Jake's face toward him, Steve saw a bloody nose. Jake's eyes fluttered open, then he vomited all over Steve.

Steve pushed Jake away. Getting to his feet,

Steve stumbled and vomited before being hit by a blinding white beam of light.

Slowly DJ came to. She was lying in a hospital bed with IVs hooked up to her arm. She was in a surgical gown. Her jeans and T-shirt were hanging off a metal rack.

"Mom? Dad?" she called out. *Where am I?* she thought. She couldn't remember anything. She smelled of sweat. She tried to focus on her surroundings. Was it the hospital? It didn't look like it. There were no windows, no TVs, no nurses. No Mom. Or Dad. It looked like she was in some kind of research lab. She lay on the bed, fighting back her panic. Machines lurked nearby and made clicking and beeping noises. She could not read the symbols on the machines. It was not English. What were they for?

She could hear approaching footsteps. *Hopefully, a nurse*, she thought.

Then she remembered looking at the dead hound and the awful smell. It was the same scent that she noticed now, wafting toward her. DJ heard a door sliding open. She turned her head and came face to face with a ghoulishly gray being. It had a large cone-shaped head and two beady black eyes. It was about three feet tall with spindly arms and legs, just like the ones in all those Hollywood movies.

It approached her slowly, extending a bony finger. Then it traced her forehead with its finger. Sweeping her hair back. It tapped her forehead. DJ fought back a scream. She was shaking.

The alien looked deeply into her eyes. It was studying her. It put its finger to her heart and thumped her chest. One. Two. Three times.

DJ let out a blood-chilling scream. Then she blacked out.

Meanwhile, Dr. Perez sat in the diner and reread the government reports and the maps. He wondered where those three college kids had wandered off to. They should have returned to town hours ago. He needed to get those samples out in the express mail by five o'clock sharp. He had no idea what was coming out of the sinkholes. A shiver went down his back. He only knew that whatever was making everyone sick was coming from the sinkholes. The pattern was clear.

Dr. Skinner had given him the coordinates of the ranch visits she had made for the diseased cattle. Plotting them on the map, he realized the ranches were within a one-mile radius of each sinkhole. Something toxic and deadly was coming from them. Something that clearly impacted livestock. He needed those guys to get him the samples, sooner rather than later.

He texted Juan, the most responsible of the

three, at least he thought so.

Dr. Perez: Estimated time of arrival? Express mail picks up in 15 minutes

Five minutes passed.

Dr. Perez: If you do not make the deadline, you will be removed from your position

Five more minutes passed. Still nothing.

Dr. Perez: Where are you?

Five o'clock. No response.

The server came up to his table and pointed to his glass. "Would you like a refill?" he asked.

"Yes. And can I get a tuna fish sandwich as well?" Dr. Perez asked.

"Sure thing."

After ordering his sandwich and packing

his reports into his briefcase, Dr. Perez glanced out the diner's front window. He'd fire those kids and send them back to Boston if they ever showed up.

Dr. Perez finished eating. There was still no sign of his three students. He checked his messages one more time. Nothing.

Losing his patience, he scrolled through the images of the sinkholes on his phone. He had received the photos of the sinkholes and the excavations from the feds. He knew that the formations were unnatural. And so did the feds. Whether the sinkholes were human-made was another story.

The first batch of the soil samples that he had sent to his colleagues in Mexico just a few days ago did not help. Those colleagues, charged with evaluating the early biological samples, were strangely mute. They had answered his emails with very short, direct replies. They claimed that the standard tests showed nothing strange. That was it. They did not draw any conclusions or offer any theories.

Dr. Perez sent a few follow-up emails to

press them for more answers, but they did not respond. In his mind, he kept going back to that one statement: "no business in carbon-based cells." That statement, though, worried him. When he told his fellow scientists, back at his home university, they tried to downplay it or bury it as if it were no big deal. But it was a big deal. In his twenty-five-year career, he had never seen any result like it.

He checked the time. Where were those students? Why hadn't they checked in with him? They hadn't texted or called. Where were the new soil samples? Did they get lost out there? Dr. Perez called 9-1-1. It was time to send someone out to find them.

As he dialed, he looked out of the diner's window again. He blinked. What in the world was walking down the street?

A ghoulish gray alien?

He rapidly snapped photos with his phone.

A group of crows circled and settled upon the high-tension power lines. DJ felt herself floating through the air like a ghost, following the flight path of the crows. The blackbirds looked at her with suspicion. They studied her. They could see she was changing. She felt like she was no longer fully human. She was becoming something else. What had the alien done to her? Did it control her brain? Her thoughts? Her movements? The alien must have injected her with a serum or implanted a chip within her brain. She did not know. Nor could she think clearly enough to remember all that had happened. Her body was not in her control. Tremors shook her body.

Then she landed on her feet on the ground. She shook again and the sparse contents of her stomach were heaved out onto the road. She did not feel right. At all. She had little information aside from her painful, pounding temples. Cold sweat trickled down her back. Then she saw her hands. They were wrinkled and gray, just like the alien.

Looking around, she vaguely recognized where she was. The diner, the pharmacy, the vet clinic. Foggy Creek. Whatever was controlling her had sent her there. With every new thing she saw, she felt a clicking in her brain as if someone were ticking off the boxes on a checklist or snapping photos. The police station. Click. The bank. Click.

DJ walked down Main Street, surveying the town. Spasms of pain racked her limbs, and soon she lost her balance. Landing on her hands and knees, she saw green ooze trickle from the scrapes on her palms. Her blood had been turned into green slime. She tried to scream, but only a low gasping moan escaped from between her cracked, dry bloody lips.

The town was eerily quiet. No dogs were barking. No children were playing soccer in the park. No cars were zipping down Main Street. It was only DJ walking down the street, her limbs feeling disjointed. She felt her eyes blink closed, then open, like the shutters on a camera. With a tremor, she rose in the air and felt her body drifting away.

DJ soared over the town. The diner. The police station. The high school. Then she was above her family's farm. She saw a pile of dead dogs. Her eyelids shut and opened. Click. Clack. A recording of some sort. Was it for someone or something else? She soared over a sinkhole. Then over a truck filled with cases and shovels. Click. Clack. She drifted to a landing at the edge of the sinkhole. It was the one closest to her house. The largest of the fourteen sinkholes.

This sinkhole was partially filled with water. It was the size of a football field. Blue flags lined the perimeter. A reminder that the people had been there. But not now. Not since the alien.

She knew that. Somehow. She felt her alien body being pulled toward an opening in the ground. It was like she was being pulled by invisible strings, like a puppet. Down into the tunnel she went. Deeper where it was dark as night.

Then, as she descended further, she saw a blinding white light. As her alien eyes adjusted, her brain registered that it was an underground city, or base. Hundreds of gray aliens marched back and forth from a disk-shaped starship to smaller underground huts. They carried cases, electronic devices, and laser weapons. It seemed as if they were preparing for battle.

DJ felt drawn to the largest of the huts. She entered. There, in front of her, sat the alien. She thought it might be the one from the hospital.

It raised its bony arm. Pointing at her, it said, "Bow."

DJ took a knee while the alien spoke.

It spoke in clipped barks and chirps, but somehow, she understood what it said.

"A conquest of the Earth, of water, of resources, and of minerals for our survival. Total annihilation of the human species. You will lead the people to me. We will kill the inferior ones." It grunted, then said, "Keep the superior ones for research. Or for slaves." The alien pointed to the door, signaling for her to leave.

As she left, she saw a large panel, like the panel on an airplane, with levers, switches, dials, and controls. DJ stopped next to the panel. The alien approached. It flipped a lever. DJ felt her body lurch forward toward the exit. Then it threw another switch on the panel. A buzzing of noise and activity sprang into action outside the hut. As she left the hut, she saw the other aliens kick into a faster mode of movement, like when she shifted gears in her family's pickup truck.

DJ's half-alien, half-human brain struggled. She felt trapped and controlled like a robot. She moved through the throng of aliens. There were pods filled with layers upon layers of humans clinging to the walls of the tunnel. They were covered in a thick, gauzy cocoon of goo.

Her brain registered something, something buried deep down within its recesses. Uncle. Clive. In the cocoon was Uncle Clive. Click. Clack. Her eyes snapped more photos, recording all in her path of vision.

Stumbling out of the tunnel, DJ dropped to her knees in the sagebrush. She stared at her wrinkled alien hands and tried to process what the alien had told her. Total annihilation of the human species. Conquest of the Earth.

A plume of dust rose. An engine rumbled. DJ looked up. A lone female got out of a car. Her eyelids snapped images of the female specimen. The female approached her at a fast pace.

"DJ!" the female shouted. "DJ!"

DJ stood. She felt a small shift in her body, her brain. Recognition. Remnants of a past self. She felt human for a split second.

The female stopped running toward her.

"Oh my—!" the female screamed. "DJ, what happened to you?"

DJ looked down at her alien body. She wore her ax-wielding barbarian T-shirt and jeans, but she knew the rest of herself was not DJ. Her brain turned over as if a switch had been flipped. A human memory of girls laughing during a sleepover flooded through her mind. Consuela. The female was Consuela.

DJ tried to speak, but nothing came out of her cracked lips. Grunts and moans. Her throat felt dry and scratchy.

Consuela grabbed DJ's hands, pulling her close to her. She was unafraid.

"They got you too." She squeezed DJ's hands. "No, no, they haven't got you completely. Your eyes. Your eyes are still green. You are still in there somewhere."

Consuela reached into her jeans pocket. "Here. Swallow this." She ripped open a small packet that had a vitamin C tablet. "This will build your immune system to fight off the alien virus." Consuela rubbed DJ's throat like she did when she had to give her dog a pill.

“Swallow. Swallow. Good,” she said. Then she led DJ to a boulder. “Sit down until the pill kicks in.”

Within twenty minutes, DJ felt her mind clear. The brain fog, the headache, the otherworldliness started to fade. Her eyes felt almost normal. The click-clacking had stopped.

“Take another,” Consuela said, helping DJ with the pill.

The second dose shook DJ to her core. She saw her alien fingers transform back to her normal fingers. Her eyelids felt human once again. She was not gray. Clearing her throat, she spoke. “Consuela. How? How did you know?” she stuttered.

“Sergeant Mark came by the diner a few days ago. He was telling folks that he saw aliens. People were going missing.” Consuela looked around, checking behind her. “No one except me believed him. I saw one looking in my bedroom window the night before.” Consuela took off the bandana around her neck. She wiped the grime from DJ’s eyes and nose. “It was freaky. Its beady eyes and bony fingers looked just like the ones in old comic books and movies. So, I got a baseball bat and have been keeping it with me day and night in case it comes back and tries to attack me."

"Then what?" DJ asked. "What about Sergeant Mark?"

"Oh yeah . . . sorry. He ran out of the diner. And no one has seen him since."

DJ shivered. She remembered the pods. Was Sergeant Mark trapped in a pod in the aliens' lair? Who else might be?

"But, but, how did you know how to bring me back?"

Consuela shrugged. "I overheard the feds talking at the clinic. There are so many people in the clinic and in the make-shift military hospital at the high school getting pumped full of fluids with IVs. They are trying to keep people alive. It's pretty scary. Anyway, the feds seem to have this, umm, theory about the aliens. Their theory is that the aliens infect humans with a virus-like organism that they bury in the dirt. When we come in contact with it in the soil, or in dust particles kicked up in the dirt, then bam! They've infected us. It makes us violently sick. And they'll destroy us. Or try to. For some reason, though, the feds think that Vitamin C seems to stop the mutant organism. At least for a little while. So the docs at the hospital are trying that now."

"How are you not infected?"

"I take a daily dose of vitamin C. Been doing that for years," Consuela shrugged. "I've got a load in my car in case you need more." She pointed to the sinkhole. "Those are the results of the aliens and their attempts to contaminate our dirt to kill us. They are basically mining. Or would it be more like farming? Except planting toxins for us to ingest instead of nutrients?" She shook her head, "Who knows? It's all so confusing and weird!"

"What?" DJ asked. Her mind felt foggy as if she were waking up from a long, strange dream.

"Yeah, the feds were whispering about holes being formed because the aliens are pretty much mining our soil. To contaminate it. Then kill us. Understand? Aliens are trying to kill us."

"I need to sit down," DJ whispered.

"Sit in my car. Get out of the heat."

They walked to Consuela's car. She turned on the ignition and cranked up the air conditioner. She passed DJ a water bottle. "Drink."

"I saw their underground base," DJ said after taking a long drink of water.

"No!"

DJ shook her head. "I did. And their leader. He is like the brain that controls them, I think. With a panel of switches and stuff."

Consuela covered her mouth. Her eyes were wide.

"I think he was controlling me. I don't know how, but I saw things differently. I could fly. But I did not control where I was going. My brain, my body. I changed into one of them."

"It's just like in those weird sci-fi books you love so much."

"Yeah. Not fiction anymore, is it? But, why me?"

"I don't know. You've always been 'quirky.' Maybe that's what the alien wanted. A quirky girlfriend?" She giggled nervously. "Who knows? Who cares? I'm just glad you are alive. And human again."

DJ was quiet for a short time. "You said they killed some humans?"

"Yes. That alien virus just made them rot away. Some faster than others."

"But some of the people they kept. They've got them in pods in that underground tunnel," DJ said.

"Are you serious?"

Nodding, DJ went on, "Yes, like they were collecting and preserving field samples."

"Oh, my goodness," Consuela said. "You must be a prime human specimen."

"I'd rather not be. We have to get those people out."

"How?"

"I don't know. Let's head to town to see who's left alive. Who can help us?"

As DJ and Consuela drove through Foggy Creek, not even the birds sang. It was like a graveyard.

"Look!" DJ said. "There's a light on in the pharmacy. Pull in!"

Consuela parked the car in front of the building. "See any aliens?"

"Nope. Let's go inside. Fast."

They hopped out of the car and ran to the front door. The pharmacy door was unlocked. They crept inside.

"Hello. Anyone in there?" DJ said. "If you are human, you are safe."

A tumble of boxes fell off the shelves at the back of the pharmacy. A small man stumbled out. "Who are you?" he asked.

"I'm DJ, and this is my best friend, Consuela." They each reached out to shake his hand.

He did the same. "Dr. Perez."

"You're not from around here," Consuela said.

"Boston," he said.

The girls nodded.

"You all right?" DJ asked.

He nodded. "I was in the café and saw an alien walk down the street. Just one. It was dressed like you, DJ. And with so many people getting sick, I came over here to get some things to protect me from the aliens and from getting sick."

"Do you take vitamins? Specifically, Vitamin C?" Consuela asked.

"Yes, a multi-vitamin every day. Plus, supplements of C, D, and E. And fish oil. And, a probiotic for my gut health."

The girls looked surprised. That was a lot of medication.

"I'm middle-aged. When you get to my age, you must look after yourself."

"Well, I guess it is probably a good thing then. You see, that's probably why you haven't met an alien demise," Consuela said. "That's about all we know. DJ was in their clutches until I found her and gave her two doses of Vitamin C."

"That's a miracle," he said.

"Yeah, but they have people trapped in pods in an underground tunnel near one of the sinkholes. We have to get them out." DJ said.

"Pods? Underground, you say?"

Nodding, DJ then filled Dr. Perez in about her alien encounter and everything she saw.

"That's the missing puzzle piece that the feds didn't tell me about." He stopped for a second. "That must have been the trace elements that they found in the first soil samples . . . alien cells . . . trace elements from another planet . . . it was the ones no one wanted to talk to me about . . . ." His voice drifted off.

"We need to act fast, Dr. Perez," DJ said, trying to snap him back to the present situation. "People's lives are at stake."

"Oh, yes. Yes, we must develop a plan."

Consuela added, "My mom might be in one of those pods. She is not here for work or at home."

"Have you seen my parents?" DJ asked her.

"No, not since you disappeared."

Fighting back a sob, DJ said, "We have got to get to the pods. I've got to find my family."

Dr. Perez paced the aisles. Then he came back to DJ and Consuela.

"Okay. How about this? First, we free the people. Next, we destroy the alien base camp. Got it?" Dr. Perez asked.

He went to the beauty aisle in the pharmacy. "Hey, bring me a bunch of shopping bags, girls. We're going to stock up."

When DJ brought him the cloth bags, he ransacked the shelves. Throwing grooming scissors, long swabs, nail files, and nail polish remover into the bags.

"Not a good time for a manicure," Consuela said, with a wry smile on her face.

Dr. Perez looked at them. "That's how we'll break open the pods. The acetone in the nail polish remover will eat away at the film on the pods and weaken them. Then, we use the grooming scissors to cut into the pods, which will free the people."

He stopped to catch his breath. "I'm guessing that when they come out of the pods, it will be like they were newborns. We'll need to clear their noses and their throats so they can breathe our air again. That's where the swabs come in. Use them to reach in and push the goo out of their throats. Oh, might as well take some tissues with us too. In case they need to blow their noses." He tossed boxes and boxes of tissues into the shopping bags. "Here, wear these gloves," he added as he tossed bags of kitchen gloves at the girls.

"This is so weird," Consuela whispered.

"It's about to get a lot weirder," he said. "Now, you said a tunnel, correct?"

DJ nodded.

"We need to blow it up," Dr. Perez said. "Because of the way it is constructed and because of its composition, it will cave in. At least it will if we use enough force." He scratched his head. "Where can one find some dynamite around here?"

"The Army Reserve Center!" DJ shouted. "My Uncle Clive goes there!"

They threw the beauty supplies into the trunk. Then Consuela drove them to the Army Reserve Center just outside of town. The gates were unlocked and wide open.

"That's strange. The gates are always closed. They are never left open," DJ said. "Should we go inside?"

"We have to," Dr. Perez told them. "If this is the only place with explosives, we have no choice."

DJ swallowed. "All right. Let's go together." She grabbed Consuela's arm. "Watch out for aliens."

They walked up to the main building. DJ knocked on the door. No answer. She opened the heavy door and they went inside. The lights were on. But the place was quiet.

They walked slowly down a hallway, peeking into various offices and storage closets. There was no one there. No one was working. No one was walking around. No one was talking on the phone. There was absolutely no human activity at the Army Reserve Center.

Rounding a corner ahead of DJ and Dr. Perez, Consuela came to a dead stop. "The aliens got them," Consuela said as she pointed to a swarm of black flies hovering outside of an office door.

"Do not go in there. Do not look," DJ warned her. "We can't do anything to help them now. They're dead." She took Consuela's hand and pulled her away from the office doorway. "We have to find the dynamite so we can save the others."

They roamed through more vacant halls, looking in bathrooms and storerooms. Hoping to find dynamite.

"It might not be housed in the main building. In fact, it probably isn't for safety measures," Dr. Perez said. "Let's check another building outside."

After searching through three smaller storehouses, the fourth building had what they needed.

The three of them stood in front of a garage filled floor to ceiling with containers labeled "TNT. Explosive."

"TNT," DJ gasped. "The mother-load."

"Let's get it into one of their supply trucks," Dr. Perez said. He took his phone out of his pocket. Using the calculator function, he mumbled, "The sinkhole is the equivalent of one football field. How deep is it? Two hundred feet . . . to dynamite . . ." He glanced up at the stockpile. "Thirty cases should do it."

"I hope we can trust your math," DJ said.

It was midnight by the time they got to the sinkhole. Consuela had her car filled with the pod rescue equipment, bottles of water, towels, and bottles of Vitamin C. Dr. Perez followed behind them in the Army supply truck loaded with TNT.

After Dr. Perez parked, they gathered around the car, making their plan.

"I don't want you kids handling dynamite—unless you absolutely must. As a geologist, I've used it a time or two. I've been trained. I am a professional."

"Fine by me," Consuela said.

"Do you two feel comfortable going into the tunnel to free the people? Meanwhile, I'll set up an explosive ring of dynamite around the sinkhole perimeter.

Without skipping a beat, DJ said, "You bet. My Uncle Clive is in there."

"My mom might be," Consuela said.

"Good. I like your courage. I will work as fast as I can. When you get the last of the people out, you run out here." Dr. Perez placed a large bundle of TNT and a lighter on the dirt next to the car. "If I am not here waiting for you, it is because I am still lining the perimeter with dynamite. You get those people out. Tell them to run, run back to town. Clear 'em out. Then, you take this bundle into the tunnel. Take it as deep in there as you can. Light it up. Then run like you've never run before." He looked straight at them. "Understand?"

"Yes, sir," they said in unison.

"Let's do this," DJ said to Consuela. "We have to end this alien invasion and save what's left of our town."

They grabbed their bags from the pharmacy and crept into the tunnel. Careful to stay in the shadows, they moved ever so closer to the blinding white light of the underground alien base camp.

"Oh!" Consuela gasped. DJ covered her mouth, shaking her head, reminding Consuela to be quiet.

They darted between the shadows like field mice. The huts came into view. DJ pointed to the largest hut and stealthily approached it.

She peered into the doorway. The alien master was seated at the far side of the hut. Its chin rested on its chest as if it were sleeping. DJ didn't waste a second. She rushed to the control panel and found the power cable. Then she pulled as hard as she could. The power cable snapped from the machine. Lights powered down. The alien awoke with a start. DJ saw its beady eyes flicker.

She ran.

When she got outside of the hut, the other alien bodies were frozen in motion. Without the motherboard controlling their bodies and their brains, they stood at attention like robots.

That was good, for the time being. They only had one alien to deal with.

"Come on," DJ said. "The pods are back here."

They raced to the deepest recesses of the cavern.

They did just as Dr. Perez said and dumped acetone all over the pods. The strong fumes made it hard to breathe. But, the acetone dissolved some of the goo.

"Now cut!" DJ yelled. "FAST!"

Then they used the scissors to cut into the

pods. Even with the help of the acetone, the pods were thick, almost like leather. Finally, they broke through one pod and then another.

"Gross!" Consuela gasped as fluid spilled out of the pod onto her clothes.

"Keep working. The alien is out there. He'll find us soon enough."

One by one, they pulled people from the pods. They found Sergeant Mark, Uncle Clive, Consuela's mom, and three young men. DJ's mom and dad were there too, even deeper in the recesses of the pod. So many of their friends from town were in the pods and even ten feds in their black suits.

DJ cleared their breathing passages. Consuela wiped their faces with a tissue.

As the people stumbled forth, coughed up bile, and regained consciousness, DJ said, "Run! Get out of here! Go!" She waved her hands and pointed toward the tunnel's exit.

The people were dazed. Consuela took DJ's mom's hand. "Come with me. Hurry!" She led the way out. The others followed them like sheep.

They reached the tunnel's exit when the alien saw them.

It flew at them, barking and hissing and spitting. It was ghoulish.

Thinking quickly, DJ reached for a bottle of nail polish remover. She flung the liquid into its face. It screamed and flailed as the acetone burned through its eyes and skin.

"RUN!" she screamed. "RUN!"

When they got above ground, Consuela shoved the people in the direction of Foggy Creek. "Get! Out! GO!" She pointed to town. "RUN!"

Snatching the TNT off the ground, DJ shouted, "I'm going in! You get them to town!"

"Where's Dr. Perez?"

"Don't know. But we don't have time. Now GO!"

Consuela rushed off, herding the people quickly toward Foggy Creek.

Looking around in the early morning light, DJ didn't see Dr. Perez or the supply truck. *Please, please*, she thought, *please have gotten the dynamite set up*. She hoped he managed to line at least some of the perimeter with TNT.

She took a deep breath and went back underground.

As soon as she was inside the tunnel, she heard the alien's screams. She ran faster toward the terrifying shrieks. "End this now," she said to herself.

When she got into the main cavern near the huts, she saw the alien. It flailed about in a violent rage. Its skin was charred. It grabbed at its eyes.

Then it stumbled toward its hut, toward the motherboard.

It's going to try to get the other aliens restarted, DJ thought. *I've got no time. Come on*, *come on.* She needed to wait until the alien could not see her. Then she'd make a run for it.

From where she was hiding, she could see the alien inside the main hut. She had to get to the spaceship now.

She bolted. Dashing up to the spaceship, in the center of its underground base, DJ stacked up the sticks of dynamite. She lit the fuses. And she ran.

She got above ground.

How long did she have until it blew? Thirty seconds? A minute? She didn't know. She just kept on running. And running.

She could see her house. Almost there. Almost there. Almost—

KABOOM!

The force of the explosion threw her into the air. She landed face down by her front porch. The wind got knocked out of her.

She gasped and rolled over. In the distance she saw rubble and debris flying. She heard booms and crashing like a huge volcanic explosion. The earth shook.

An Army supply truck barreled toward her house. Dr. Perez!

She jumped up, gasping for breath, and frantically tried to wave him down.

He slammed on the brakes. "Get in! Get in!"

DJ sprung into the cab.

He cranked the truck into gear and high-tailed it to town.

"Did you line the whole thing?" she asked, catching her breath.

He nodded. "You better believe it. Just in time too." He turned onto the highway. "Who EVER said geology was boring?"

The dust had settled. DJ, Consuela, and Dr. Perez stood near the pile of rocks and rubble. Just six short hours ago, they had freed people from alien pods and ignited a literal truckload of dynamite, destroying an alien base camp.

"Amazing, isn't it?" Dr. Perez asked. "The explosions caused a chain reaction, filling in the sinkhole and burying the aliens and their base."

"It's over," DJ said, slightly amazed.

"We're safe," Consuela said. "They can't destroy our town, or us, anymore."

DJ let out a long sigh of relief. Her family, thank goodness, was safe and sound. Consuela's mom was okay. Even Dr. Perez's students, Juan, Steve, and Jake, were fine after they were rescued from the pod. Many of the town's residents were too, although lots of people, pets, and livestock did not make it. They'd have to have burials soon. There would be lots of sadness and trauma to deal with. Foggy Creek would never be the same.

DJ's house, despite being so close to the blast, survived intact, with just a few broken windows.

"I am so thankful," DJ said to Dr. Perez and Consuela. "For both of you. And for being alive." She started to cry. Waves of shock and relief washing over her.

Consuela leaned over and gave her a hug. "We decimated those aliens. They won't be messing with planet Earth again."

"I hate to interrupt you, ladies, but we need to meet Sergeant Mark at the sinkhole on the opposite side of town in fifteen minutes. Hop in the truck." Dr. Perez went to the supply truck and started the engine. "Feel like moving some more dirt?" he shouted from the cab.

Consuela smiled. "Does it involve more dynamite? Because if it does, count me in!"

At a smaller sinkhole across town, Sergeant Mark walked the perimeter. Dr. Perez was behind him, measuring and placing sticks of dynamite at equal intervals. Consuela and DJ were busy taking photos of the sinkhole. They wanted to document at least part of the events. Too bad it was without the aliens. Folks would just have to take their word for it and believe them—without photographic evidence.

"They're going to blast all of the sinkholes," Consuela said as she posted an image of the sinkhole to her social media account. "Destroy any trace of alien existence."

"Don't you think people will come snooping around? Especially after you post online."

"Probably," she said. "The feds will fence them off, no doubt. Maybe they'll post 'DO NOT ENTER' signs. That kind of thing."

Laughing, Consuela added, “But that never stops the die-hard alien hunters.”

DJ shook her head. “I can’t believe any of it. And I lived through it. I was there.”

Dr. Perez called out to them. “Hey! Bring the lighters!”

Consuela and DJ went into action. They grabbed the lighters and they sprinted to Sergeant Mark and Dr. Perez.

“Give us old-timers time to get back to the truck. When we do, you light ‘em up and run back to us. We’ll kick it into gear and haul out of here,” Sergeant Mark said.

Off they went, running around the sinkhole, lighting the fuses, until they circled back to the truck.

“Hop in!” Dr. Perez said. He shifted and hit the gas.

They crashed across the dirt, putting distance between them and the dynamite. “And—NOW!” he yelled.

BOOM!

The explosion propelled the truck forward

about a hundred yards. They landed with a bone-jarring thud.

"Two down!" Sergeant Mark said. "I'll radio the feds and tell them it worked. Time to blast the others!"

The federal agents had positioned themselves by the remaining sinkholes. They had their professional explosive teams. They were ready.

One by one, DJ could see the blasts, the debris, and the smoke fly into the air.

Consuela counted them out loud. Finally, she said, "That's it. Every. Last. One."

Thirteen Black Hawk helicopters roared overhead. Each went toward a different sinkhole.

"Checking the progress," Sergeant Mark said. "Making sure they got it done." He patted DJ on the back. "Nice work, kiddo."

"Thanks."

Three Months Later

Federal agents, the men in black suits, still roamed Foggy Creek. They were keeping out the riffraff, DJ's mom said.

Not long after the sinkholes were blasted with dynamite and filled with debris, the feds went to work there. DJ saw concrete truck after concrete truck haul loads out to the area by her family farm. They were pouring concrete into and over the sinkholes. So, not only were the sinkholes filled with debris and rocks, they were then covered by concrete. *Talk about thorough*, she thought. Nothing will ever come out of that ground again.

The feds built massive walls and constructed barbed wire fences around each sinkhole. They installed security cameras and posted signs. "GOVERNMENT PROPERTY. KEEP OUT."

DJ texted Consuela.

DJ: About ready to head out.
See you in five days!

Then she grabbed her duffel bag and got into the pickup truck. She smiled when she saw Consuela text back.

Consuela: Have fun and happy 18th birthday! We'll celebrate when you get back. Drive safely! Go get those prize-winning bulls!

DJ revved the engine of the pickup truck.

She blasted the horn. Her dad sprinted out of the house, suitcase in hand. Her mom was close at his heels.

"Wait up, wait up," she said, carrying a plastic container of food.

Her dad climbed into the cab, tossing the suitcase behind his seat. "Hey, DJ! Happy birthday!" He leaned over and gave her a peck on the cheek. "So glad those aliens left the McMullin's bulls alone in Denver." He chuckled. "Got the checkbook? We're going to go invest in our future!"

She nodded and flipped open the lid of the center console, pulling out the checkbook. "Let's get the best of the best," she said.

Knocking on the driver's side window, her mom held up the plastic container. "Cupcakes, for the road, for my birthday girl."

"Thanks, Mom."

"Love you, honey." Mom waved goodbye.

"Love you, too."

"Hit the road," dad said, smiling proudly. "We've got some distance to cover today if we want to make it to Denver tomorrow."

DJ stepped on the gas, and they drove off. She ended up graduating high school shortly after they defeated the aliens. But instead of heading off to college right away, she decided to spend one more year home. She'd work on the family ranch, hoping to bank some money before heading off to college and spend more time with friends until they graduated.

She calculated how much she needed to save for her first year. It was a lot between tuition, books, food, and housing. She could do it, though, if the ranch did well. And if she lived off beans and rice. After blowing aliens to smithereens, she could do this. Her dad always told her: Sacrifice today to have a better future tomorrow. That was the plan.

As DJ drove, she noticed the walls and signs around the sinkholes, blocking them off from outsiders, alien hunters, and prying eyes. The feds didn't want leaks about the alien invasion to circulate. *Too late*, DJ thought as she drove. Photos of an alien DJ had popped up on social media. Posted by "anonymous science guy." Who could've taken a photo of her in her alien form? She didn't know. Nor did she really care. The aliens were destroyed. Her friends and family were alive. Let people say what they will. She knew what really mattered.

DJ turned onto Main Street. Dr. Skinner's vet clinic had a flashing sign on the corner of the street: "We treat all creatures. Great and small. But not aliens." The diner now had a huge alien statue on its roof. The high school had changed its mascot to the Intergalactics, a gray alien. Even the pharmacy had an alien painted on its window with a sign that read, "Our customer service is out of this world."

DJ smiled. What a weird, wonderful world she lived in. And she was thankful for that.

ABOUT THE AUTHOR

Ronald B. Kline, Jr. is a science teacher who has a passion for writing. He has a BS in Biology from USF and a master's in educational leadership from Nova Southeastern University. By 2023, Ron will have served as a teacher in the Hillsborough Country School District for thirty years. He is married with two children and lives in Florida.